The Three Marys

Fiction by Lynn Coady
Hellgoing (2013)
The Antagonist (2011)
Mean Boy (2006)
Saints of Big Harbour (2002)
Play the Monster Blind (2000)
Strange Heaven (1998)

LYNN COADY

The Three Marys

GOOSE LANE EDITIONS

"The Three Marys" previously appeared in the 1999 anthology *Home for Christmas: Stories from the Maritimes and Newfoundland* and originally, in a different form, as part of Lynn Coady's 1998 novel, *Strange Heaven*, both published by Goose Lane Editions.

Up in the hospital's teen lounge were bruise-eyed thirteen-year-olds who sat with IV skeletons behind them, cutting holes into folded pieces of white paper for gluing the shapes together to make bells, candles, and holly. Once these were finished, the craft lady would string a piece of gold thread through the top, because they were to be sold at the Christmas Craft Fair — all proceeds going to the Hospital for Sick Children — as tree ornaments.

Bridget was there, too. She and the rest of them from Four South — the Psych Ward — were being forced up daily to create their own individual masterpieces. Byron complained about it. He said it was hideous and "Dickensian" to force these children, who uniformly wanted to lie down and die, into the lounge to listen to Burl Ives and toil on a felt-and-glitter production line. Nurse Gabby told him that a lot of the children found doing crafts to be therapeutic.

"What about those of us who don't find it therapeutic, but a sadistic torment?"

"Some people don't know something will be therapeutic until they try it," Gabby soothed, shooing the herd of them into the elevator.

If Bridget got any pleasure from seeing Byron hacking a swastika out of green felt to the tune of "Holly Jolly Christmas," it was only when she looked at him alone, and not at the others sitting in a row with them at the long table. The sight of them made her think that he was right. Dying children shouldn't be expected to make Christmas ornaments out of felt. People would buy them at the craft sale and put them on their trees: Look! An actual dying child made this manger. We understand it was cystic fibrosis. And here's our leukemia candy cane. And we got this wreath from the Indian reservation.

There was no denying that some of them probably did enjoy the diversion, or were at least being diverted by it. One translucent fourteen-year-old — whom Bridget, with her new-found expertise, would have diagnosed as anorexic, but later learned had full-blown AIDS — had a particular flair for the decorations. She could even twist the felt in elaborate ways to give the finished product a three-dimensional effect, and the craft lady would always hold her latest creations up for everyone else to be inspired by and talk about the new dialysis machine or surgical laser it would help the hospital to buy. The girl would sneeze, picking up another wad of felt and eating glue off her fingers.

Bridget was another of the craft lady's stars. Sick of the felt and glitter, she had been looking through some of the lady's craft books and come across what looked like a fairly easy method of making lovely, ornate snowflakes simply by curling strips of white paper and gluing them together. She soon found out that it wasn't easy to do at all. It was extremely intricate work, and it took Bridget four days of her teen-lounge time to complete the first one, which by all accounts was a masterpiece. The craft lady exhorted her to come up with at least five more before the sale, so Bridget began taking her work downstairs to the ward with her. The snowflakes required tremendous concentration. Bridget worked on them every spare moment, which in her present mode of existence meant practically all the time. Gabby and Dr. Solomon could not have been more supportive of this new interest, Bridget's first and only interest since being admitted.

It seemed to make Solomon all the more certain that her decision to send Bridget back home for the holidays was the right one. For the first time since informing Bridget of her discharge, on report of the snowflakes, Solomon came round the ward to view Bridget's handiwork.

"These are just lovely."

"Ya want one?"

"I'd love to have one. And maybe you could donate a couple for the ward's tree."

"Take your pick."

"Thank you, Bridget. You've got a wonderful eye. I'm sure you'll do very well in pottery."

"Pottery," said Bridget, looking up.

"Have you enrolled at the college yet?"

"No. I guess I better do that, eh?"

"I would think so. It must be getting rather late."

"Yeah, I'll do it."

"Are you looking forward to going home?"

"Oh, I dunno."

"I'm sure your family will be glad to have you back. Your Uncle Albert especially."

"Albert doesn't even live with us."

"Oh!" The doctor moved her electrolysed

eyebrows slightly. "I was given to understand that he did. He was so insistent you be sent home."

It was because Albert liked for people to be where they goddamn well belonged. He had been harassing the entire ward ever since Bridget's arrival. Gabby told her this. Gabby had related that sometimes he would call up on the pretext of wanting to speak to Bridget and instead take the opportunity to blast whichever nurse had picked up the phone.

"Hello, Four South."

"Is Bridget Murphy there, please?" Polite, older-male-relative voice.

"Yes, if you'll hold a..."

"Well, Jesus liftin', when are you fag psychiatric sons of whores gonna let her out of that hellhole?"

"Would you like to speak to Bridget, sir?"

"I'd like to speak to her all right. I'd like to speak to her sitting in her own goddamn kitchen is where I'd like to speak with her, but I can't do that until you bastards decide to turn her loose — as if she's some kind of Jesus menace to society or something."

And the nurses, being psychiatric nurses, wouldn't be as quick to respond in the same way that someone else in the same situation might — namely by hanging up on the raving old fart. They were psychiatric nurses who had been trained for every eventuality, and this sort of thing they were eternally ready for. The family was a volatile thing. The family — usually the organism responsible for the child's internment in Four South in the first place — could not normally be expected to comprehend why one of its number would need to be there. Bridget gathered that phone calls like Albert's were more or less par for the course in Gabby's line of work. Leaning back into the chair and lighting a cigarette, whichever nurse was on shift would robotically switch into a mode of soothing rationality once the first note of hostility reached her ears.

"It's not that she's a menace to society, sir, that's not the case at all. It's just that she needs a bit of sheltering right now."

"Shelter she can get from her family!"

"No, obviously not, or she wouldn't be here."

"What the eff is that supposed to mean?"

"I only mean that your daughter has come through a hard time, and often, following events as overwhelming as a pregnancy and adoption, a young woman will need a period of ... hibernation, if you will..."

"She's not my goddamned daughter."

"Oh. To whom am I —"

"This is her uncle, by god! Albert Patrick Murphy!"

"Well, Mr. Murphy, we do appreciate your concern —"

"Yah, well, you may as well appreciate me hole for all the good it does."

Bridget often thought her uncle must be unique. He was the only man she knew who saved his temper for strangers rather than his family and friends, and not the other way around. When she'd lived with him and Bernadette in the late summertime, Albert would curse at the TV news and its single mothers ("welfare sluts"), simultaneously leaning over to pour Bridget more tea and berate the little bastard who was her undoing.

"You're a good girl," he would tell her over and over again. "You're a good girl and a goddamn smart girl and no little puke from Home Hardware is going to mess up a future as bright as yours, good girl." Bridget tried for a couple of minutes to envision it, a future as bright as hers.

Her father was a craftsman. Once, he had worked for the government, had practically run the town at one point, but residents soon became appalled at the kind of upheaval he was constantly trying to achieve. He had wanted to build a senior citizens' home, for one thing. He had wanted "Causeway Days" — the spring festival — to attract more tourists, to entail more than a five-float parade down the main street, two of which were furnished by the mill, three of which were no more than locals in toilet-paper-decorated pickups with signs on the front reading stuff like "Jimmy Archie's Lumber" or "Come to Dan Hughie's Garage. Two for 99 on O Henrys."

Bridget's father had also wanted some kind of musical event other than the traditional bagpipe contest that had led him to refer to the festival as "Catkilling Days" during an interview at the local radio station. Many residents had been offended. They were proud of the bagpiping contest. It was one of the many things that made the community unique. They found Mr. Murphy to be overbearing and unduly aggressive. One day her father came home late from a meeting and announced, "Piss on 'em. They can play the bagpipes until their foolish lungs implode. I hope they all go deaf as me arse." And he went downstairs to work on his craft.

Woodworking was his craft. He called it that, but it was really more like art. Nobody dared suggest this to him. Once a TV station out of Halifax had called him up to be on some program about Maritime folk art. "I'm not some kind of dope-smoking hairy-faced fruit," was what he'd said. "Unlike you and yours." Television was television to her father — Halifax no different from Los Angeles. "Ar-teests," he'd spit, whenever the subject came to mind, making flitting gestures with his short, yellow fingers. "Arse-tits is more like it."

So her father was a craftsman of wood. He drove off into the hills every Sunday to pick choice pieces. He especially liked the trees that had some kind of disease that made the trunks bulge monstrously out in places, as if gourds had become lodged in there somehow. Her father would take the diseased trunks home and carve all sorts of faces into the bulges. If there were a lot of bulges, the effect was very much like that of a totem pole — caricatures of bulbous-nosed hobos and sailors replacing those of owls and wolves and ravens. Big-nosed, heavy-lidded men's faces were one of her father's specialties.

At other times, he would come home with what appeared to be an average piece of wood, spend a few hours sanding and varnishing it, and then present it to the family — a smooth, polished piece of wood.

"Whaddya think of that?"

"It's really nice!"

"Do you see what it is?"

"Um. A fish?"

"It's a wolf's head. See, there's its snout. By god, nature does the work, I just bring it to the fore."

Mr. Murphy also delighted in any chunk of wood that bore a passing resemblance to parts of the human anatomy. He stole a pair of Bridget's mother's shoes once to put on a branch that had been uncannily like a bum and a pair of legs — right down to having little protrusions where the feet would be. This was where he hung the shoes. Bridget's mother got mad because they were good shoes, but he wouldn't let her replace them with a pair of old slippers or anything. He referred to the artifact, for some reason, as Mrs. MacGillicutty, and pretty soon, after he had returned gleeful from the woods one day with what he said was a husband for Mrs. MacGillicutty, Bridget's mother wouldn't go down to his shop any more.

The shop did a fairly good business because he made cabinets as well, and because he overpriced his artwork outrageously, for the tourists. He had also acquired a reputation for being a character, and local people were always stopping by to see what he'd do. They found his insults endearing, but if they ever loitered too long, he'd bark. "If you're not buying, you're leaving," in such a way as to make the people fear that they had offended him somehow. In such a way as to prompt them to buy, perhaps, one of his twenty-five-dollar golf balls. With those, he peeled away half of the ball's pitted skin and then carved more goofy faces into the hard rubber beneath. Everyone thought this was ingenious.

What a lot of people really came for, though, were Bridget's father's decoys. His decoys were simply beautiful, more perfect than any actual duck. They were entirely smooth and flawless — he did not bother with feathers or any other realistic detail that might disturb the decoy's linearity. The result was a perfect, liquid platonic ideal. Perfect duckness. He stained — never painted — and then varnished them. The wood was what mattered, the acknowledgment and refinement of the wood, as opposed to any attempt to deny it, that was what made the carvings very nearly sublime. People came from far and wide to purchase one of Bridget's father's ducks. They were all exactly the same.

When Bridget got home from the hospital, there were two pieces of news right off. One was that the trial of the girlfriend-murdering Archie Shearer had finally gotten under way, and the other was that her father had taken to bringing Rollie down to the basement with him, and now Rollie was an artist, a craftsman, too.

Rollie's school had been shut down. Rollie used to go to a special school every day where he would make bread with other adults like himself. The bread was very good, and Bridget's mother bought loaves of it every week. It spoiled the family for the store-bought kind, and on weekends, if they ever ran out, Gerard would sometimes go on rampages, rummaging through the deep freeze in the hope of finding a forgotten loaf, hollering, "Where's the retardo bread?"

Rollie loved going to school, and if Bridget's parents ever wanted to punish him for not going to bed when they told him to, or taking a piss out of doors, or pulling his shorts up over his belt and ripping them, then they wouldn't let him go. It was a very effective punishment, and they were relieved to finally have discovered some kind of leverage to use against him. It was widely acknowledged within the family that Grampa and Margaret P. had spoiled Rollie most of his life — cutting his meat and pouring his tea and putting his mittens on for him — and so when it came time for Rollie to live under Bridget's father's rule, Rollie knew how to be quite stubborn. Bridget's father didn't know any way to make him do anything except for cursing at him and giving him the occasional shove up the stairs. It was still a little difficult with Margaret P. around. Sometimes Rollie would stumble into her room in tears, and Margaret P. would bang on the wall with her bedpan, wanting to know what had been done to him.

"Jesus Murphy, Ma, I was just trying to get him to take off his own goddamn shoes!"

"He's never had to take off his own shoes, for the love of God!"

Bridget's father saw that changes had to be made, so he sent Rollie to the "special school" as soon as it opened up. And Rollie surprised everyone by loving it. He had even managed to acquire something like a girlfriend, a woman named Emma, overweight and smiling. Every night before going to bed, Rollie would ask Bridget's father, "Who's going to wake him up see Emma?" — and her father would revel in his new-found power.

"Well, now, I don't know if anyone should wake you up for school tomorrow, not coming in for supper when Joan calls you."

"He'll come in for supper."

"You will, eh? You're not going to do that

again, walking around in circles going No no no no like a Jesus lunatic?"

"No, he's not."

"You're going to come in next time, then, are you?"

"No he's not, no he's not," Rollie would say rapidly, putting his hands over his ears.

"Well, are you going to come in next time or aren't you?"

"He's going to come in next time."

"All right then. Go on up to bed."

"Who's going to wake him up for school, Raw-hurt?"

"Robert will wake him up for school."

But now — due to lack of resources — Rollie's school was shut down. It was a trying time for everyone. Bridget's father didn't know what was to be done with Rollie during the day. He sat in his chair with the television on and would complain. "When's Rollie going to school see Emma?" every time Bridget's mother or father went by. This, along with his constant inquiries over the last few months about where Bridget had gone, was combining to drive the two of them up the wall. So one day Bridget's father announced, "Shit on this. You come downstairs with me, sir. We'll get you going on something."

This was how Rollie became an artist. Not just an artist, but, according to Bridget's father, a religious artist, the best kind of artist to be. Her father had stuck a piece of wood into Rollie's hand and let him go at it with the sander. So Rollie stood there, humming to himself and sanding and sanding the wood until Bridget's father took it away from him and held it up to the light. There and then he declared the overly sanded block of wood to be uncannily — one might say miraculously — representative of the Virgin holding the baby Jesus. He ran upstairs to show it to Bridget's mother and asked if she agreed, and Bridget's mother said that she supposed so, and so he hurried back down to the basement to varnish the new work and put it on display, stopping only to hand Rollie another piece of wood to get started on.

According to Bridget's mother, Rollie was becoming famous. Her father had a whole display of his religious carvings lined up on the shelf above the golf balls. Little cards in front of each announced what the wooden blobs were supposed to represent, from "Jesus Heals the Sick" to "Saint Paul on the Road to Damascus." Some people who visited the shop seemed initially dubious about the carvings until Mr. Murphy explained who had done them. He daringly set them at the same price as his carved golf balls, a great favourite among locals and tourists alike, and, in a flash of inspired business savvy, put up a bigger sign above them all which read:

> Religious Wooden Statues.
> Done by Retarded Man.
> Twenty-five Dollars a Piece.

And now they were her father's number-one seller. Even more than the ducks. They were especially popular with Christmas being on its way. Bridget's father, in anticipation of the season, had glued sprigs of plastic holly to the occasional piece.

That, and the trial of Archie Shearer for murdering Jennifer MacDonnell in August, only now beginning. Now. At Christmas, people emphasized. Sad for the family, they said, meaning the MacDonnells. And the thought of sad families at Christmas inevitably brought to mind that of the self-slaughtered Kenneth MacEachern from down the street. The state of the local young people was freshly lamented around Bridget's kitchen table. So much unhappiness brought upon the families. Killing each other and killing themselves.

The visitors, coming round the house all through the holidays, said that. There was teensy

Mrs. Boucher, Margaret P.'s old housekeeper, rasping between drags on her DuMauriers and kicking her dangling feet, which never reached the floor when she sat down. She always kicked them back and forth like an impatient six-year-old.

"It just make me sick," she would mourn, "all de deat." Mrs. Boucher was a mournful woman, sickly, with a sad life. She'd sip her tea, everybody aware of her fear for her married nineteen-year-old girl, in and out of the women's shelter every two or three months. Everyone in the house found themselves wanting to get things for Mrs. Boucher.

"I tell her, come home with me, Louise. No, Ma, I rather get the crap beaten out of me than live with my mudder like a little kid. Well, what do you do?"

Uncle Albert, down with Bernadette for the holidays, would nod soberly even though he wasn't. Bernadette reported that Albert was "back at it again," after thirty-three years. No one could really believe it. Apparently he had turned up with a bottle of Crown Royal one day last week and ecstatically poured himself three fingers in front of his wife.

("What in the lord's name are you about with that?" I said to him.

"To hell with it," he says. "It's Christmas, the kids are all gone, and I've been sober for thirty-three years. It's time to celebrate, Mommy!" And doesn't he gulp the Christly thing down in front of my eyes!)

Now, everyone sort of had the feeling that they should behave very disapprovingly and discouragingly toward Albert every time he came out from underneath the sink with his bottle shouting, "Who wants a snoutful?" — but with the exception of Bridget's father, no one could actually bring themselves to do it. He was too much fun. Except for putting him in perpetual good cheer and turning his cheeks and nose a welcoming pink, the liquor had no great effect on the man, certainly none of the adverse effects that everyone, for some reason, had been expecting. He was simply the same old Albert, spreader of good cheer, offering to replace poor Mrs. Boucher's tea with a hot buttered rum.

"No, it no good for my stomach, Ally."

"Ach, it's good for every goddamn piece a ya. A nice toddie then, Marianne?"

"No, Albert, no, I just have more tea."

Which meant Albert had to content himself with making a toddie for the priest, whom he did not approve of half as much as he did Mrs. Boucher, a woman who had spent six years of her life caring for Margaret P. in spite of her own hardships. Bridget could remember being small and sitting at the kitchen table at Margaret P.'s house with Mrs. Boucher, watching her smoke and listening to her ghastly stories about her no good brudder. Her no good brudder used to break into her apartment and steal the television set for booze. Her no good brudder would threaten to beat her if she didn't give him money. Mrs. Boucher said back then that she was so relieved to be working at Margaret P.'s, away from her no good brudder, that she was almost sick.

Bridget remembered trying to keep up by telling Mrs. Boucher about Gerard, who always beat her up and spit in her hair and wouldn't play with her. He had gotten hold of her Wonder Woman doll and sawed the top of its head off with his pocket knife.

Albert was in a state that Bernadette cluckingly called "High Gear" — scuttling around to make toddies for himself and sleepy, pink Father Stewart, another harmless and uninteresting drunk, and then darting down the hall to check on Margaret P.'s cheer, which lately hadn't been too bad. Margaret P. had taken to singing the song about the three Marys since Bridget got home, and despite the depressing lyrics, the singing seemed to keep her content and less likely to succumb to her usual macabre hallucinations. When Bridget first showed up, Margaret P. had been convinced that Bridget herself was one of these spectres, having returned from the dead after being shot by a boy. Margaret P. thought Bridget was Jennifer MacDonnell. Or else thought Jennifer MacDonnell had been Bridget. But this notion didn't seem to frighten Margaret P. in the least. She said, "Hello, dear. Are you still in purgatory?" and began to say a rosary. Since then, every time Bridget stopped into Margaret P.'s room, the ancient thing would say nothing beyond holding up the rosary, shaking it encouragingly and calling — as though Bridget were far away — "It won't be long now, dear! You just hold on a bit longer."

"I'm not in purgatory, Gramma."

"We'll get you up there, dear. I've lived a good life and they'll listen to me."

But now Margaret P. had forgotten about the continual rosaries and taken to singing "Mary Hamilton" all day long. She sat, rocking back and forth and singing about the three Marys over and over again, a smile nestled somewhere in the folds of her face. She only remembered the one verse.

> Yesterday e'en there were four Marys.
> This night there will be but three.
> There was Mary Beaton and Mary Seaton.
> And Mary Carmichael and me.

Albert and Bridget's father were pleased to hear the old lady singing after so long, but only Bridget seemed to recognize that Margaret P. had confused it for the rosary, that in her cobwebby mind she was still busy praying for Bridget's unworthy soul. And she must have considered it pretty unworthy because she hadn't stopped since Bridget got back.

Albert had been explaining all this to the priest and Mrs. Boucher — how Margaret P. had gotten it into her head that Bridget had been shot instead of Jennifer MacDonnell, and as yet no one was able to convince her otherwise — and this was what set them off on the subject of the dead, bemoaning particularly the young people, and all the dying and killing they did.

"It's the parents!" Albert pronounced recklessly. High Gear had the effect of causing Albert to make several reckless pronouncements throughout the day. Ideas he might otherwise have made every effort to suppress in front of Bridget's father.

"It's not the goddamn parents," the latter countered at once. "I've never bought into that psychiatric free-love save-the-seals horseshit and I'm not about to now. Blame everything on the parents, forget about personal responsibility. I say if some little bastard is gonna be a weirdo goon and pick up a rifle to shoot some young girl stupid enough to get tangled up with him, then that's what he's gonna do. And people encourage that now, anyway. They think its cool to be wanting to do away with themselves or the young girls. It's in the videos they watch. Well I say let them kill themselves if they want to, but if they start aiming those guns at anyone else, by God, I'll hold the door to hell open for them and kick their arses through."

Bridget's mother said: "Well, I didn't know Archie Shearer, but Kenneth MacEachern was in my religion class and he was just a lovely lad. He told me he wanted to be a priest."

"Oh, yes, but the sons of bitches change once they hit their teens," Bridget's father said, happy to be angry and deliberately not checking his language in front of Father Stewart. "They get arrogant and start thinking they know everything, and you can't tell them a goddamn thing after that."

All the proof he needed of this was, Bridget supposed, sitting at the table with him. He had made his disgust at both her and Gerard's respective betrayals known since the first day they had ever disagreed with him. Gerard had been about thirteen, Bridget a couple of years older, and their father had been so offended that he hadn't bothered to try and tell them anything since. Now if he ever wanted to express displeasure at something they did, he pretended to agree with it, not speaking to them, but to the air. "Yes, that's what he wants to do," he would say. "He figures it's the right thing. Well by the Jesus, why doesn't he do just that? Why the hell not? Goddamn, if that isn't just a dandy one." Gerard could imitate their father at this with uncanny accuracy.

Bridget had to reacclimatize herself to all the

chaos she'd forgotten about, especially now that she had the empty, echoing ward to contrast it against. She had read somewhere that people who are colour-blind all their lives find it too overwhelming, once their eyes are operated on, to experience the world in colour. They lose all perspective and are terrified and lost and sometimes get physically sick. That's what coming home was like, even though Bridget had spent all her life there and only four months on the ward. Coming out was a far greater adjustment than going in had been.

She would sit and drink tea until about three in the afternoon and then switch to rum and eggnog before dinner, wine during, and anything else went for the remainder of the evening. She could get away with this because it was Christmas and because everyone wanted her to be happy. She was genuinely pleased at how much easier it was to get drunk after four months' abstinence, although it was not the same kind of drunk as before. It made her serene, content to be doing whatever thing it was she happened to be doing. If she was baking cookies with her mother, she was content to be doing that. If she was helping Margaret P. to the toilet, she was content to be doing that. Because her feeling was that really she wasn't doing that. This was a relief. She didn't get edgy and excited like she used to, and have to leave the house at two in the morning.

And nobody chastised her, about anything. Her father did not even confide his displeasure to the air.

"What about you, Bridget? Didn't you know Kenneth? Or was it Archie Shearer you knew?"

Her mother had always been one to forget about unspoken household rules. Her father said she did it on purpose. Once, when he had decided a few years back that he was going to disown

Uncle Albert, and made it understood that no one in their family was to have any contact with him, Joan had forgotten all about this edict in the second week and ruined the effect by calling up Bernadette to make plans for a day of shopping at the Mic Mac Mall. So Bridget shouldn't have been surprised, really, that her mother would conformingly tiptoe around her for the first couple of days, clearing away teacups, before absently letting drop a question about killing and dying.

"Bridey's one of the good ones, goddammit!" Albert interjected, pink-faced and reckless. She could hear the recklessness in his voice as he stood at the counter behind her, and she could feel everyone willing him to sit down and have a piece of bannock or something.

"God only knows she could have taken the easy way out, or done something foolish or what-have-you," he came up behind her chair and Bridget could hear him swallow. She looked up at Gerard, who sort of smiled. He was leaning on his hand, fingers tapping against his head as if they were feeling for a trap door.

"We should just thank the lord she had enough sense to do the right thing!" Albert finished in an even louder voice than he started with.

"Yes, Bridget, you're a wise girl," Father Stewart agreed, being priestly in his attempt to save Albert from awkwardness.

"Goddamn right!" Albert barked, repaying the father with blasphemy. He gave Bridget a pat on the head which was too hard.

Bridget's father looked at Albert for a little while to make sure he was finished speaking. "That isn't really what we were talking about, now, is it?" he said, at length. "That's not what I would call the issue at hand. I believe what we were talking about was a lot of jeezless punks who should all be sent to military school. That'd straighten them all out pretty damn quick. They'd take that heavy-metal horseshit, the army would, and all those big ideas about the world and how they should all kill the parents who feed them and grow their hair to their arseholes and be a bunch of faggots who don't have children but want to adopt normal people's and eventually kill off the whole goddamn human race, the army would sew all that horseshit up into a tight little ball, stick it in a rifle and fire it straight up their arse, that's what a little discipline would do for those sons of whores."

"Oh, now," said Father Stewart, rousing himself a little. "My."

Between four and six in the morning, Bridget would dream she was still on the ward, packing to go home. She was feeling around in the ceiling tiles, where she used to hide money and Mars bars and the like from the staff, looking for her stuff, but none of it was there. Instead she kept pulling out handfuls of all these nonsensical items, all this crap. Car alarms, even though she wasn't really sure what a car alarm would look like. Plain doughnuts. The filter out of her mother's clothes dryer. The head off a Barbie. And one morning at about eleven o'clock Bridget came downstairs to pour herself a cup of tea, and her mother told her she had already come down four hours earlier. Bridget didn't believe her. Joan had said that Bridget had looked her straight in the eye and demanded: "Where the hell is it?"

"It's up in bed, dear," Joan had supplied without batting an eye. Maternal telepathy.

"Up in bed? Are you sure?"

"Yes, it's up in bed, dear, go on up."

"All right then!" Bridget supposedly had said, stomping back up the stairs.

Bridget's father had given her a couple of Rollie's statues. One blob was supposed to represent the Virgin and another was the Virgin and Child. It was ironic, but she knew he didn't mean it to be.

When she and Gerard were children, her father always made sure that there were one or two religious pictures hanging on both their walls. Bridget always got the Virgin, the Baby, or the Virgin with the Baby, whereas Gerard always got a grown-up Jesus doing stuff — cleansing the temple, showing Thomas the holes in his hands and whatnot. Her father had this idea that girls liked Mary and boys liked Jesus, just as girls liked Barbies and boys liked GI Joes. So he had picked out the Madonna blobs for Bridget merely on the assumption that they were the most appropriate choices. Gerard got "Jesus Heals the Sick."

"There," he said. "You two go upstairs and pray to those for a little while, see if that doesn't do ya any good."

Bridget put them on her nightstand, which was where he would be looking for them, and prayed vaguely for no dreams. Then she had a nightmare about the Christmas turkey, the first frightening dream she'd had since, probably, the first trimester, when she went around punching herself in the gut and doing sit-up after sit-up after sit-up. Her father had just cut into the bird when it leaped off the table, still hot and crackling from the oven, screaming, "Don't you dare! Don't you dare!" Trailing stuffing across the kitchen floor.

photo: Rob Appleford

LYNN COADY's *Strange Heaven* was nominated for the Governor General's Award for Fiction and the Books in Canada First Novel Award, and won the Dartmouth Book Award and the Atlantic Booksellers' Choice Award. She has since written three novels, *Saints of Big Harbour*, *Mean Boy* (which won the Georges Bugnet Award for Fiction), and the Giller-nominated *The Antagonist*, all national bestsellers. She has also written two books of short stories, *Play the Monster Blind* and *Hellgoing*, which won the 2013 Scotiabank Giller Prize. Her non-fiction has appeared in *Canadian Geographic Traveller*, *Hazlitt*, and *Chatelaine*. She is co-founder and editor-at-large of the award-winning magazine *Eighteen Bridges* and divides her time between Edmonton and Toronto.

Copyright © 1999, 2014 by Lynn Coady.

All rights reserved. No part of this work may be reproduced or used in any form or by any means, electronic or mechanical, including photocopying, recording or any retrieval system, without the prior written permission of the publisher or a licence from the Canadian Copyright Licensing Agency (Access Copyright). To contact Access Copyright, visit www.accesscopyright.ca or call 1-800-893-5777.

Series edited by Martin James Ainsley.
Cover and series design by Chris Tompkins.
Art direction and page design by Julie Scriver.
Printed in Canada.
10 9 8 7 6 5 4 3 2 1

Library and Archives Canada Cataloguing in Publication

Six@sixty / edited by Martin James Ainsley.

Short stories compiled to commemorate Goose Lane's sixtieth anniversary.
3. The three Marys / Lynn Coady.
Issued in print and electronic formats.
ISBN 978-0-86492-853-5 (set : pbk.).— ISBN 978-0-86492-793-4 (set : epub).—
ISBN 978-0-86492-858-0 (v. 3 : pbk.).— ISBN 978-0-86492-734-7 (v. 3 : epub).

I. Ainsley, Martin James, 1969-, editor. II. Coady, Lynn, 1970- . Three Marys.

PS8321.S59 2014   C813'.010806   C2014-902978-0
                                            C2014-903186-6

Goose Lane Editions acknowledges the generous support of the Canada Council for the Arts, the Government of Canada through the Canada Book Fund (CBF), and the Government of New Brunswick through the Department of Tourism, Heritage, and Culture.

Goose Lane Editions
500 Beaverbrook Court, Suite 330
Fredericton, New Brunswick
CANADA E3B 5X4
www.gooselane.com

This book, typeset in Minion Pro
and Gill Sans, was printed and bound in Canada by
Friesens in Altona, Manitoba, on 55 lb. Rolland Enviro
100 FSC Natural Antique.